A Sparrow's Magic

by MARIA NIKLEWICZOWA

pictures by FUYUJI YAMANAKA

English version by ALVIN TRESSELT

PARENTS' MAGAZINE PRESS • NEW YORK

This book was translated from *Suzume No Mahou*, published by Kaiseisha Publishing Company, Tokyo, Japan. The American edition has been arranged through Nippon Shuppan Hanbai K. K., Tokyo.

It had been a long cold winter in the forest. All through the snow and ice the hamster had slept deep in his snug warm house.

Now at last the spring had returned, and he woke up. He stuck his head outside and sniffed the soft air. "Oh," he said as he stretched, "after a long sleep I am so hungry!"

He quickly scooped up some of his stored wheat and went outside to eat in the warm sunlight.

He had no sooner started nibbling away when a quail walked by. "Good day, Mr. Hamster," she said happily. "I'm so glad to see you are up.

"Today is my birthday, and I would like you to come to my party. We will have dancing and games and good things to eat."

This pleased the hamster very much, and he was just about to say he would be happy to come, when the quail added, "There's just one thing, though. I have no flour to bake a cake. Would you let me have some of your wheat?"

Now the hamster was rather greedy and he said, "Oh, no, I couldn't do that. I have scarcely enough for myself."

"Very well," replied the quail crossly. "Then you needn't bother coming to my party." And she quickly flew off.

When she arrived home, there was the mouse waiting to see her. "Dear Miss Quail," he began, "I have to write a letter, and I can't find my quill pen anywhere. Would you give me one of your fine long feathers?"

"Certainly not," she replied, for she was still feeling cross. "The weather isn't settled yet, and I need all my feathers to keep me warm. Now run along. I have lots of work to do."

"What a selfish bird she is," said the mouse to himself as he started home. "She has plenty of feathers. Surely she could have spared one of them."

Suddenly he heard the sound of crying. There by the side of the path he spied a baby rabbit caught in a trap. He was sobbing bitterly and kicking his free foot up and down.

"Please help me," he cried when he saw the mouse. "If I don't get out of this trap the hunter will come and catch me."

"I'm much too busy to help you," answered the mouse. "I have to hurry home to write a very important letter. If you had watched where you were going, you would not have gotten caught." And the angry little mouse scurried on home, even though he knew he couldn't write his letter without a pen.

In the meantime, the hamster had eaten until he was quite full. Now he began thinking about the quail's party. "How foolish I was," he said. "I should have given her the wheat. Then I could have a good time dancing and playing games. Maybe I'll just go over and peek at what's going on."

Suddenly he realized that his feet were cold, so he decided to visit Mrs. Rabbit first and see if she would make him some shoes of soft rabbit fur.

But when he got there he found Mrs. Rabbit in a terrible state. Without even asking what the trouble was, he said he would like her to make a pair of shoes for him.

"How can I think of making shoes," she replied. "My little boy went off into the woods and hasn't come back. Will you help me look for him?"

"My feet are much too cold for me to go running around looking for a lost rabbit," said the hamster.

"Well!" said Mrs. Rabbit. "If that's all you care about my baby I won't make you a pair of shoes." And off she hopped to look for her child.

Now the quail was still very angry about her spoiled party when a little sparrow flew by.

"Why are you looking so upset, Miss Quail?" he asked.

"Oh, it's that hamster," she said. "He wouldn't give me a few grains of wheat so I could bake a cake for my birthday party."

"Let me see what I can do," said the sparrow, and he flew off again.

Next he saw the mouse, and he, too, looked sad and upset. "What seems to be your trouble?" asked the little sparrow. The mouse explained about the selfish quail who wouldn't give him a feather so he could write his important letter.

"I'd be happy to give you one of mine," said the sparrow, "but I'm afraid it would be too small. Let me see what I can do." And off he went.

He hadn't flown very far before he heard the baby rabbit crying. "Help me, help me," pleaded the rabbit. "The hunter will soon be here to catch me. I asked the mouse to chew the rope, but he wouldn't do it."

"I can't chew rope," replied the sparrow. "But be patient. I'll see what I can do."

At last the sparrow came to the hamster's house. "Well, Mr. Hamster," he said, "what are you doing in your house on such a fine day?"

"The ground is still cold, and I have no shoes to keep my feet warm," he answered. "And Mrs. Rabbit refused to make a pair for me."

"Mrs. Rabbit is very kind. Why wouldn't she make them for you?" asked the sparrow.

"She had to look for her lost baby," replied the hamster. "And she expected me with my cold feet to help her."

Now it was the sparrow's turn to get angry. "Mr. Hamster," he said, flying up and down in the air. "It seems to me there are a lot of selfish, unkind creatures in this forest. And you are the one who started it all. You wouldn't give the quail any wheat, she wouldn't give the mouse a feather pen, the mouse wouldn't let the rabbit out of the trap and Mrs. Rabbit wouldn't make you a pair of shoes because you wouldn't help her look for her baby. Now let's see if we can straighten things out," he went on. "First, give me enough wheat so the quail can bake her cake. Then we'll see what happens after that."

Feeling very ashamed of himself for having caused so much trouble, the hamster gladly gave the sparrow the wheat.

Miss Quail was so pleased. "Now we'll have a lovely party after all," she said. Then she pulled out one of her prettiest feathers and gave it to the mouse.

The happy mouse was about to run home to write his letter when he remembered the baby rabbit. He hurried over to the trap and with a few nibbles of his sharp teeth he gnawed through the rope and freed him.

The mother rabbit was overjoyed to see her baby again. She gave his ear a little pull just as punishment for running off, then she gave him a warm bunny hug to tell him she loved him. That reminded her. "I must quickly make a pair of shoes for Mr. Hamster so his feet won't be cold," she said happily.

That afternoon the quail had a fine birthday party and everybody came. They were all good friends again, and they all agreed it was the best party they had ever been to. The cake, of course, was delicious.

"Kindness is the best magic of all," said the sparrow to himself as he watched the happy animals enjoying themselves.

The hamster in his new warm shoes danced round and round with the quail, while the mouse tried to teach the little rabbit how to dance without stepping all over him with his big feet.

"Happy birthday to you, Miss Quail," said the hamster gayly. "Your party was such a lovely way to welcome spring."